First edition 2021

Library of Congress Catalog Card Number pending
ISBN 978-1-5362-0732-3

20 21 22 23 24 25 CCP 10 9 8 7 6 5 4 3 2

Printed in Shenzhen, Guangdong, China

This book was typeset in Agenda Medium.
The illustrations were done in mixed media.

Candlewick Press
99 Dover Street
Somerville, Massachusetts 02144

www.candlewick.com

SHEEPISH

(WOLF UNDER COVER)

helen yoon

CANDLEWICK PRESS

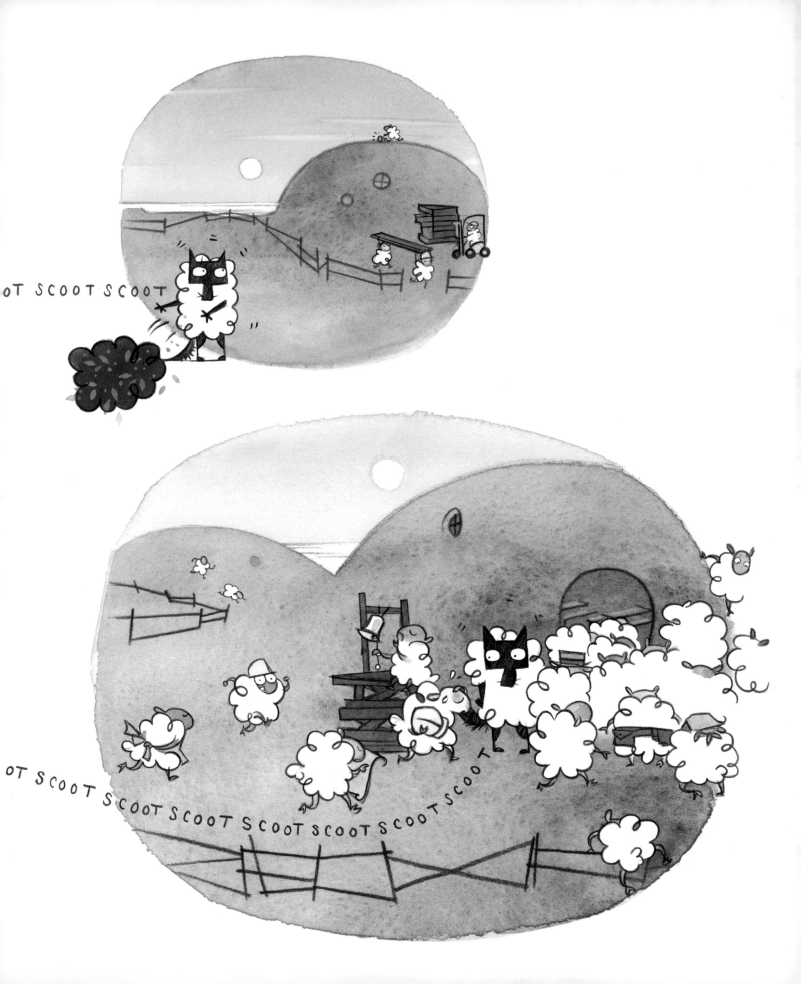

Success! I'm in!

Shhh!

I'm pretending to be a sheep.

Nobody suspects a thing!

It's all part of my master plan.

Step one: Be helpful.

Step two: Be handy.

Step three: Be fun, be friendly,

be a team player.

Step four: Be the sheepiest
sheep that ever was.

Then, when they least expect it,

dinnerti—

Huh?

I can't do it!

NOPE NOPE NOPE NOPE NOP

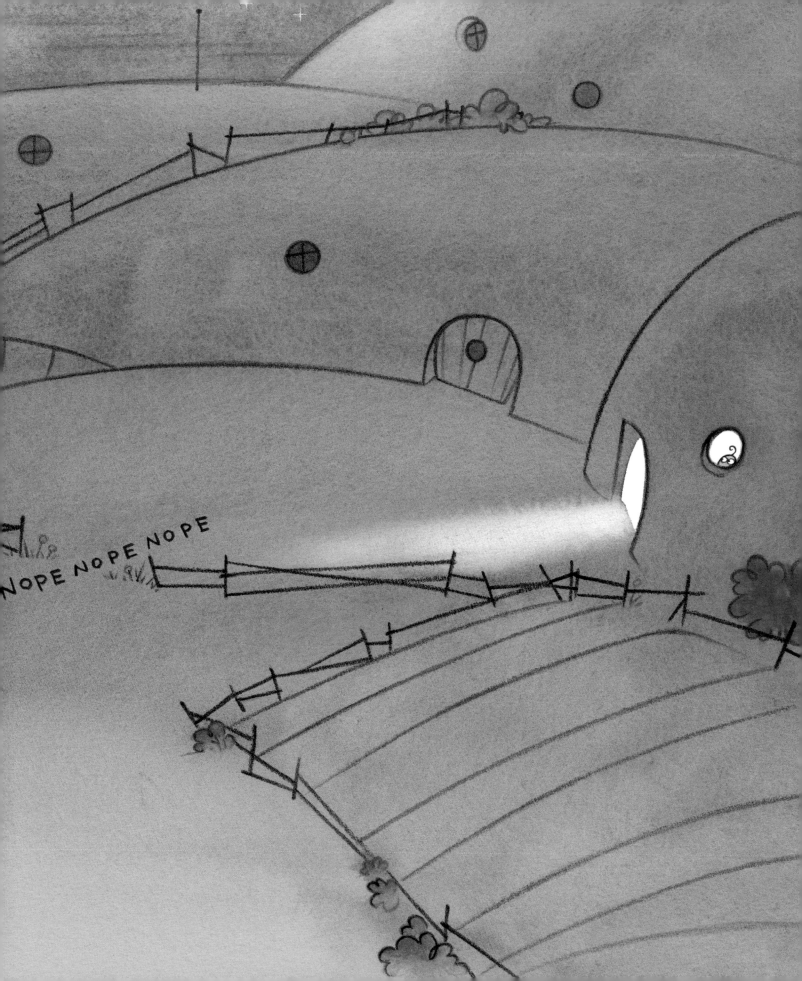

New plan.
Step one.

Step two.

Success.

"You knew?"